by ABBY KLEIN

illustrated by
JOHN McKINLEY

Scholastic Inc.
New York Toronto London Auckland
Sydney Mexico City New Delhi Hong Kong

To my family,
I love our new tradition of going to the apple orchard every year and picking our own crisp, juicy apples!
—A. K.

ISBN 978-0-545-13045-5

12 11 10 9 8 7 6 5 4 3 2 1 10 11 12 13 14 15/0

Printed in the U.S.A. 40
First printing, July 2010

Apple Orchard Race

#1: Tooth Trouble

#2: The King of Show-and-Tell

#3: Homework Hassles

#4: Don't Sit on My Lunch!

#5: Talent Show Scaredy-Pants

#6: Help! A Vampire's Coming!

#7: Yikes! Bikes!

#8: Halloween Fraidy-Cat

#9: Shark Tooth Tale

#10: Super-Secret Valentine

#11: The Pumpkin Elf Mystery

#12: Stop That Hamster!

#13: The One Hundredth Day of School!

#14: Camping Catastrophe!

#15: Thanksgiving Turkey Trouble

#16: Ready, Set, Snow!

#17: Firehouse Fun!

#18: The Perfect Present

#19: The Penguin Problem

#20: Apple Orchard Race

CHAPTERS

I have a problem.

A really, really big problem.

My class is going on a field trip to an apple orchard. There is a wooden apple hidden in one of the trees, and the first person to find it wins a prize. I want to win, but Max is such a bully he will do everything he can to stop me.

Let me tell you about it.

CHAPTER 1

Red Shirt Alert

Brrrriiiiinnnnng! Brrrriiiiinnng! My alarm clock rang. I grabbed the clock and was about to throw it across the room when I remembered that today was a special day. I put the clock down and jumped out of bed.

I yanked off my pajama shirt and pulled open my T-shirt drawer. I started throwing shirts on the floor and muttering to myself, "Where is it? Where is it? It's got to be in here somewhere."

I couldn't find it anywhere, so I ran into

the bathroom. My sister, Suzie, was in there combing her hair. She combs it for about twenty minutes every morning, like she's some princess.

"Get out! Get out right now, Shark Breath," she screamed at me.

"I'll be out in a minute," I said. "I just have to find something."

"Well, why don't you put on a shirt, Weirdo?"

"I will as soon as I find it."

"Find what?"

"My red shirt!"

"What's so important about your red shirt?"

"My class is going to Apple Hill Orchard today, and Mrs. Wushy said we should all wear something red."

"What about your underwear with the big red hearts on it?" Suzie said, laughing.

"Very funny," I said. "I don't have underwear with big red hearts. Besides, you have to wear something red that everyone can see. People don't see your underwear!"

I started throwing things out of the dirty-clothes hamper.

"You can look for your shirt when I'm done," said Suzie.

"I don't have time, Sleeping Beauty," I said. "I can't be late for school, or I'll miss the field trip."

I threw a few more things out of the hamper. By now there were dirty clothes all over the bathroom. I didn't see my shirt, so I started to run out when Suzie grabbed my arm.

"Hey, get back here," yelled Suzie.

"Get back here? I thought you wanted me out."

"I do, but what about this mess? You know Mom hates it when there are dirty clothes on the floor. She is going to be really angry."

"You can clean it up."

"Oh, no! That's your job, mister," Suzie said. "You made the mess. You clean it up. Besides, I'm not touching your dirty underwear."

"But I don't have time. I can't be late, or I'll miss the bus and the field trip. Please just help me out."

"What's it worth to you?" asked Suzie.

I didn't have time for this. "Just tell me what you want," I said.

"I get to use your handheld video game player for a week."

"A week? Are you crazy? I play that on the bus every morning."

"I know," Suzie said, holding up her pinkie for a pinkie swear. "So do we have a deal or not?"

I thought about it for two seconds, and then I held up my pinkie. "Deal," I said as we locked pinkies. I really didn't want her to have it for a week, but if I had to clean up the bathroom, I'd miss the field trip.

I turned and ran out of the bathroom, down the stairs, and into the kitchen. "Good morning, Freddy," said my mom. "That's a very interesting outfit you have on today."

My dad looked up from reading the newspaper and chuckled. "I'm pretty sure a shirt is required at school. It's not the beach, you know."

"I know. I know," I said. "But I can't finish getting dressed until I have my red shirt."

"Why not, honey?" said my mom.

"Remember, my class is going to Apple Hill Orchard today, and Mrs. Wushy said that we have to wear something red. The only red thing I have is that T-shirt Grandma bought me for Christmas. I have to find it," I said, jumping up and down. "I just have to."

"OK, OK, calm down," said my mom. "Did you look in your T-shirt drawer?"

"Yes," I said.

"I bet it's in the bathroom," said my dad.

"No, I looked there, too."

"Maybe it's in the laundry room," said my mom. "I did do a load of laundry yesterday."

"Can you check? Can you check?" I said, jumping around in my pajama bottoms.

My mom left the room.

"You look like a monkey, jumping around like that," my dad said, laughing.

"And you smell like one, too," Suzie said as she walked into the kitchen.

"Suzie, that's not very nice to say to your brother," said my dad.

"Well, he is a stinky monkey," Suzie said, sitting down at the table.

"Suuuzieee," said my dad. "You need to apologize to your brother."

"Fine. Sorry," Suzie said. I knew she didn't mean it, but I didn't have time to argue. I had to find that red shirt, or I was going to miss the bus.

"Mom, do you see it?" I yelled.

Just then my mom came back into the kitchen. "Sorry, Freddy, it still needs to be washed. But I found Suzie's red sweatshirt and your favorite shark T-shirt. Will that work?" she asked, holding up the sweatshirt.

"OK! Thanks, Mom. You're the best," I said, giving her a big hug.

"Well, Freddy, you'd better run back upstairs

and finish getting dressed," said my mom. "You don't want to get on the bus half-naked."

"No!" I laughed. "That would be REALLY embarrassing!"

I ran upstairs, put on my shirt and the hooded sweatshirt, and went flying back into the kitchen. "Now I'm ready!" I announced.

"Um . . . aren't you forgetting something?" said Suzie.

"For your information, I am wearing underwear."

"Ewwww. That's not what I meant, Hammerhead. Look down."

I looked down at my feet. I had on my fire truck slippers. "Oops," I said, my face getting warm.

"I know you're supposed to wear something red, but if Max saw those, he might never stop laughing," said Suzie, smiling.

"That would be an interesting trip to the orchard, in your slippers," my dad said.

"Oh yeah," I said. "That was a close one. I'd better go change." I ran back up the stairs, two by two. I got back down just in time to grab a breakfast bar and my backpack, and head out the door to hop on the bus.

CHAPTER 2

An Apple Surprise

When we got to school, our teacher, Mrs. Wushy, said, “You all are going to have a great time today. We’re going to do lots of fun things at the orchard.”

“Oh, yeah?” said Max. “Like what? Apples are boring.”

Mrs. Wushy ignored him and kept talking. “We get to pick apples, see how a real cider press works, and eat cider doughnuts. They’re my favorite!”

“I love them, too!” I said. “They are so yummy!”

“I can’t wait to try them,” said Jessie. “I’ve never had one before.”

“You always have such a good attitude about everything, Jessie,” said Mrs. Wushy.

“Yeah,” I whispered to Robbie. “Not like Mr. Grumpy Pants over there.” I pointed at Max.

Max looked up just in time to see me pointing.

I gulped. Oh no! The biggest bully in the whole first grade was not supposed to see me pointing at him.

"I'll get you later," he mouthed at me.

"I'm in trouble now," I whispered to Robbie.

"Don't worry about it," said Robbie. "He just likes to act tough."

But that didn't make me feel any better.

"When we get there, do we have to walk all

the way up to the apple trees?" Max asked. "I've been there before, and it's a long walk up to the trees. I don't want to walk that far."

"Actually," said Mrs. Wushy, "you don't have to walk at all. When we're ready to pick the apples, Farmer Bob is going to give us a hayride over to the apple trees. That's a special treat just for us."

"A hayride!" said Jessie. "I've always wanted to go on a hayride. I just love horses."

"Ewwww," said Chloe, holding her nose. "Horses are stinky, and the hay is really prickly."

"You're just a prissy princess," said Max.

"No, I'm not!"

"Yes, you are," said Max.

"No, I'm not," said Chloe, folding her arms and pouting.

"All right, you two," said Mrs. Wushy. "That's enough."

"Can I ride the bus up to the apple trees?"

Chloe asked. "My mom told me to keep my dress clean today. It's brand-new. My nana just brought it to me from France."

"Why would you wear a brand-new dress to a farm?" Jessie whispered to me.

"Because you're Chloe," I whispered back.

Jessie giggled. "I forgot. She's a princess. Princesses don't wear pants."

"And they don't ride in hay carts," said Robbie. "They ride in carriages."

"No, I'm sorry, Chloe," said Mrs. Wushy. "Everyone is going to go on the hayride."

"B-but . . . ," Chloe stammered.

"No buts. Those are the rules. And speaking of rules, what do you think are some important rules to remember today?" said Mrs. Wushy.

Jessie raised her hand.

"Yes, Jessie?" said Mrs. Wushy.

"Don't touch anything until Farmer Bob says it's OK."

"That's right," said Mrs. Wushy. "You have to

listen to Farmer Bob and do exactly what he tells you to do."

I raised my hand.

"Yes, Freddy?"

"No screaming on the bus."

"Good. Remember you need to use a quiet voice on the bus and stay in your seat. Anything else?"

Robbie's hand shot up. "I know the most important thing," he said.

"Great! Tell us," said Mrs. Wushy.

"You should always stay with the class and never walk off by yourself."

"That is an excellent rule," said Mrs. Wushy. "Why do you think that is so important?"

"Because if you leave the group, you might get lost," said Jessie.

"Ooooh, that would be scary," said Chloe, pretending to shiver. "I would not want to get lost in the orchard. What if they couldn't find

you, and it got dark, and you had to spend the night outside in the dark all by yourself?"

"Well, we don't have to worry about that," said Mrs. Wushy, "because no one is going to wander off. Right, kids?"

"Right!" we all said.

"Now that you have promised not to wander off, I'm going to tell you about a special surprise."

"Special surprise!" we all chanted. "Tell us what it is!"

"Farmer Bob has set up a little treasure hunt for us."

"Cool!" I said.

"Yeah. Way cool," said Robbie.

Even Max was sitting up and listening.

"Here's how it's going to work," said Mrs. Wushy. "Farmer Bob has hidden a wooden apple somewhere in the orchard. When you are out picking apples today, you have to keep your eyes open for it."

"What does it look like?" asked Chloe.

"A banana," Robbie whispered to me. "What does she think it looks like?"

"It looks just like a real apple, except it's made out of wood," said Mrs. Wushy.

"That sounds tricky," said Chloe.

"If it looked different from all the other apples, then it would be too easy," said Mrs. Wushy. "It might be a little tricky, but I know someone will find it."

"What happens if you find it?" asked Jessie.

"You get a prize," said Mrs. Wushy.

"What?" said Max. "An apple?"

“No,” said Mrs. Wushy. “You get five dollars!”

“Five dollars! Wow! That’s a lot of money!” we all said.

“So is everyone ready to go?” said Mrs. Wushy.

“Yes!” we answered.

“Then grab your coats and line up at the door!”

CHAPTER 3

Cheater, Cheater, Pumpkin Eater!

When we got on the bus, Robbie and I sat down next to each other in a seat. Jessie sat right across from us. The minute Max stepped onto the bus, I whispered to myself, "Don't sit near me. Don't sit near me," but of course he had to take the seat right behind me.

"Great," I whispered to Robbie.

"Well, look who's here," Max said, leaning over the seat and sticking his face in mine. "It's Baby Freddy."

"Freddy is not a baby," said Jessie.

"Says who?" said Max.

"Says me," said Jessie. "Don't you remember he slid down the fire pole on our field trip to the fire station? Babies don't do that!"

"Right," said Robbie. "I didn't see you do that, Max."

"Well, I've done it before," said Max.

Just then Mrs. Wushy said, "Everyone needs to sit down so that the bus can start moving."

Max started to say something, but Mrs. Wushy walked by and asked him to sit back down in his seat.

The bus started to pull out of the school parking lot.

"I'm so excited to go to the orchard," said Jessie. "I've never been to one before."

"You're going to love it," I said. "It's so much fun to pick the apples right off the tree."

"And wait until you taste one," said Robbie.

"A fresh apple from the orchard is much better than one from the supermarket!"

Jessie licked her lips. "I think I can taste it already."

Chloe turned around in her seat. "What are you eating? There is no eating on the bus. That was one of the rules."

"For your information, Miss Busybody," said Jessie, "we aren't eating anything. We were just talking about apples."

"Oh," said Chloe.

"You know what's the best thing to make with fresh apples?" said Robbie.

"Apple crisp!" I said.

"No! Applesauce," said Robbie. "Every year my mom makes homemade applesauce with the apples we pick from the orchard."

"I don't think I've had homemade applesauce before," said Jessie.

"I'll bring you some to try," said Robbie. "It's delicious!"

"Well, my mom makes the best apple crisp with the apples we pick every year," I said. "In fact, one year she even won first prize at the fall festival for her apple crisp."

"That sounds yummy, too," said Jessie. "Is it like apple pie? Because I love apple pie with vanilla ice cream."

"It is a lot like apple pie," I said. "I like the apple crisp when it's warm and the ice cream melts just a little bit."

"Hey, guys, can we stop talking about this?" said Robbie. "It's making me hungry!"

We all laughed.

"I know what you mean," I said.

"What should we talk about?" asked Jessie.

"I know," I said. "How about the treasure hunt?"

"That sounds so cool," said Robbie. "I think it will be hard to find the apple, though."

"Why?" I said.

"Because it is going to be really well camouflaged."

Robbie is a science genius, and he always uses these big words. "Um . . . could you speak English please, Einstein? What does 'camouflaged' mean?"

"It means it's the same color as its environment, so it blends in really well and is hard to see."

"You mean like how the design on a butterfly helps it blend in with the flowers?" asked Jessie.

"Exactly," said Robbie.

"I have really good eyes," said Jessie. "I bet I can find the special apple, even if it is camouflaged."

"Not if I do first," I said.

"Dream on, Ding-Dongs," said Max. "You haven't got a chance."

"Why not?" said Jessie.

"Because I'm going to find it first."

"Oh really?" said Jessie.

"Yeah, really," said Max.

Chloe turned around in her seat. "You're such a bragger, Max. The only way that you will find it first is if you cheat, and we all know that you are a cheater."

"I am not!" Max yelled.

"Oh, yes, you are! Every time there's a contest, you cheat!" said Chloe.

"I do not!" yelled Max.

"Yes, you do!" said Chloe. "You're a cheater, cheater, pumpkin eater!"

Max jumped out of his seat and was about to grab Chloe when Mrs. Wushy stopped him. "Max, you need to go back to your seat and sit down right now," said Mrs. Wushy.

"But . . ."

"Right now!" said Mrs. Wushy.

Max plopped back down into his seat with the help of Mrs. Wushy.

"Now, what is all the yelling about?"

"She called me a cheater," Max said, pointing to Chloe.

"Because he is," said Chloe.

"That's not very nice to say, Chloe," said Mrs. Wushy. "Would you please tell Max you're sorry?"

Chloe just stared at Max.

"Chloe, I'm waiting," said Mrs. Wushy.

"Yeah, and I'm waiting," said Max.

"I'm sorry," Chloe whispered.

"What did you say?" asked Max. "I didn't hear you."

"Sorry," she barked, and slid back down in her seat.

"Now, I don't want any more yelling," said Mrs. Wushy, "and, Max, you need to stay in your seat. Understand?"

"Yes," mumbled Max.

Mrs. Wushy walked back to the front of the bus. "We are almost there, boys and girls," she said. "If you look out the windows right now, you can see the sign for Apple Hill Orchard. We just turn right here, drive up that road, and we'll be there. In fact, I think I see Farmer Bob waiting for us at the top of the hill. Get ready for an apple adventure!"

CHAPTER 4

Farm Perfume

The bus came to a stop right next to an old barn, and we all started to get off. Max pushed and shoved his way to the front so that he could be the first one off. He ran up to Farmer Bob and accidentally stepped on his foot.

"Slow down there, buddy," said Farmer Bob. "Good thing I have these boots on or you might have squished my toe! What's the rush?"

"I'm going to find the wooden apple and win

the prize," said Max. "Can we go now? Can we?"

"You have to be patient. We're going to do that a bit later," Farmer Bob said, chuckling.

"Patient! I don't think he knows what that word means," Robbie whispered to me.

I laughed. "He definitely does not."

"Max, Farmer Bob is going to give us a little tour before we go up to the orchard. Why don't you come back here and stand with me?" said Mrs. Wushy. She took Max's hand and pulled him to the back of the group.

"How many of you have ever had apple cider?" asked Farmer Bob. Some kids raised their hands.

"My mom only buys the fresh, organic kind at the Natural Foods Market," said Chloe.

"Well, you can't get any fresher than the cider we make here," said Farmer Bob. "We have our very own apple cider press right here on the farm, and we use it to make fresh apple cider every day. Would you all like to see it?"

"Yes! Yes!" we said.

Farmer Bob took us all into the old barn, and we walked over to a big machine.

"What's that?" asked Jessie.

"That's the cider press," said Farmer Bob.

"It looks really old," I said.

"It *is* really old," said Farmer Bob. "My grandfather built it, and he used it to make apple cider right here on this very farm."

"Wow!" said Robbie. "It must be like fifty years old."

"Oh, it's older than that, but we haven't changed it a bit. We still make apple cider just the way he did over fifty years ago."

"How does it work?" asked Jessie.

"Well, you dump the fresh apples in here," said Farmer Bob. He lifted Jessie up so she could see into the big bin.

"What's in there?" we all asked.

"A whole lot of apples!" Jessie said, laughing.

Farmer Bob put Jessie back down. "Then this part here chops the apples up into pieces and spits them out onto these screens."

"That looks like the screen on my bedroom window," said Max.

"That's exactly what it's like," said Farmer Bob. "The apples get squished between these two screens. The juice comes out, but the apple pieces get stuck in the screens."

"Where does the juice go?" asked Robbie.

"It goes into these pipes," said Farmer Bob, "and then gets stored in that big cooling tank over there until we are ready to put it in jugs."

"What do you do with all of the leftover apple pieces and apple skins?" Jessie asked. "Throw them out?"

"Oh no!" said Farmer Bob. "Come with me, and I'll show you."

We followed Farmer Bob out of the old barn and across the path to the pigpen and horse stalls.

"Oh, P.U.!" Chloe said, holding her nose. "It stinks over here. I think I'm going to be sick."

"I call that farm perfume," Farmer Bob said, laughing.

"I call that P.U. stink!" said Chloe. "My nana brought me real perfume from France, and that is not perfume!"

"Seriously, I can't believe she's making such a big deal about horse poop," said Robbie.

Just then Jessie started giggling.

"What's so funny?" I asked.

"Look!" she said, pointing to Chloe's fancy red shoe. "I think she stepped in some . . . some . . ."

"Some what?" said Chloe.

"Some poop!"

"Oh no! Oh no!" Chloe wailed. "Get it off! Get it off! These are my brand-new shoes!" She started running around in circles.

"Calm down, Chloe," said Mrs. Wushy. "Come with me, and I'll help you wash off your shoe."

Mrs. Wushy took Chloe by the hand, and the two of them went to find a hose.

"As I was saying," said Farmer Bob, "we don't

just throw out the leftover apple pieces and apple skins. Can you guess what we do with them?"

"Feed them to the horses and pigs?" said Robbie.

"That's right," said Farmer Bob. "Pigs will eat just about anything, and my horses love the taste of those sweet juicy apples."

"It's good for the environment, too," said Robbie. "You're not putting all of that trash in a landfill."

"Everybody wins," said Farmer Bob. "You get fresh cider, my animals get fed, and we all take care of the Earth."

"Can we taste the cider?" said Jessie. "I've never had it before."

"Of course you can!" said Farmer Bob. "But first I want to take you all up to the apple orchard, so we can pick some apples to make a nice fresh batch of apple cider. Would you all like to do that?"

"Do what?" Chloe said. She and Mrs. Wushy had just gotten back from cleaning up her shoe.

"Go to the orchard to pick apples," said Jessie.

"Yes! Let's get out of here," said Chloe, "before I step in anything else." She started to walk away.

"Wait just a minute," said Farmer Bob. "I have to go get my hay cart and Sugar."

"Sugar? What do you need sugar for?" Robbie asked.

"Not the kind of sugar you eat," Farmer Bob said, laughing. "Sugar is the name of my horse. She's going to pull the hay cart."

He disappeared around the back of the horse stalls and returned a minute later sitting on top of Sugar, who was pulling a large cart filled with hay. "Hop on, everybody, and Sugar and I will give you a ride up to the orchard!"

"Awesome!" I said as I jumped onto the back of the cart.

"I've always wanted to take a hayride," said Jessie.

"This is going to be so much fun," said Robbie.

"Watch out, everybody," said Max. "Here I come!" He took a flying leap and landed face-first in a pile of hay.

"Ouch! That had to hurt," whispered Robbie.

"That's what he gets for being such a show-off," said Jessie.

"I don't think I can get up there," Chloe whined.

"Oh please," said Jessie. "I bet if she didn't wear those fancy shoes, it would be a lot easier."

"I'll help you up," said Mrs. Wushy. She lifted Chloe up and plopped her down on a pile of hay.

"Owww!"

"What's wrong?" said Mrs. Wushy.

"I'm getting poked by a piece of hay."

Mrs. Wushy just rolled her eyes.

"Everybody ready back there?" Farmer Bob asked.

"Ready!" we all said.

"All right. Hold on tight. Here we go!"

CHAPTER 5

Apple-Picking Time

The hay cart bounced along the dirt path toward the orchard.

"This sure is a bumpy ride," said Robbie.

"I would be a lot more comfortable if I had a pillow to sit on," said Chloe. "This hay is prickly."

"You think you're so fancy," said Max. "Well, guess what? You're not the queen, so just be quiet!"

Chloe stuck her tongue out at Max, but he just laughed at her.

"Sugar is such a beautiful horse," said Jessie. "She looks just like the white horses in fairy tales."

"I wish I could ride a horse," I said. "It looks like so much fun."

"It is," said Robbie.

"You got to ride on a horse?" I asked.

"Yeah, one time we were on a vacation in California, and my mom took us to a place where you can rent horses for the day and go on a trail ride. It was awesome!"

"You are so lucky. I don't think my mom would ever let me ride a horse. You know she's such a neat freak. She doesn't like anything dirty or stinky, and horses are both of those things!"

"If you look that way," said Farmer Bob, pointing, "you can see the apple trees right up ahead."

"Good," said Chloe, "because I can't sit on this hay one more minute."

Farmer Bob pulled on the reins, bringing Sugar to a stop, and we all jumped out of the hay cart. Well, everyone except for Chloe, who had to be lifted down by Farmer Bob.

Max started to walk toward the trees. Farmer Bob grabbed him by the back of his pants and stopped him in his tracks. "Hang on there, buddy. Where do you think you're going?"

"To find the wooden apple!" said Max.

"Well, if you're going to pick apples in my orchard, then you have to follow my rules, and rule number one is you don't wander off by yourself."

"Remember, we talked about that this morning," said Mrs. Wushy. "We said that you have to stay with the group. Remember, Max?"

"Yeah, yeah," Max mumbled.

"If you can't follow the rules, then you won't

be able to go," said Mrs. Wushy. "Do you think you can follow Farmer Bob's rules?"

"Yes," said Max.

"First of all," said Farmer Bob, "I have to give each of you a bucket."

"A bucket? What's that for?" asked Jessie.

“To collect your apples in,” said Farmer Bob. “I need each of you to collect ten apples in your bucket. Do you think you can do that?”

“Yes!” we all said.

“If you each collect ten apples, then we can use some of them to make fresh cider, and you can take the rest home. Follow me over here to this tree, so I can show you how to pick the apples.”

“We already know how to pick apples,” said Max.

“I want to show you the Apple Hill Orchard way,” said Farmer Bob. “Come on over to this tree right here.”

We all followed him to the tree. “You see this apple?” he asked.

We all nodded.

“You don’t just want to take it in your hand and yank it off the branch.”

“You might break the branch or hurt the tree,” said Robbie.

"That's right," said Farmer Bob. "You want to hold it gently in your hand and twist it off like this." He gently twisted the apple and it fell off into his hand. "See how easy that is?"

"What about the contest?" said Max.

"Maaaaax," said Mrs. Wushy, "please let Farmer Bob finish."

"Oh yes . . . the contest," said Farmer Bob. "Here's how it works. When you're out in the orchard, keep your eyes open wide, because I have hidden a wooden apple in one of the trees. If you find that apple, then you win a prize!"

"Five whole dollars!" said Max. "And I'm going to win it!"

"What makes you so sure?" said Jessie.

"Watch me!" said Max.

"I think that five dollars will be all mine," said Jessie.

"No way!" said Max. "There's no way a girl is going to beat me."

"We'll see," Jessie said, smiling.

Max scowled at her, but Jessie just kept smiling. She was the only one brave enough to stand up to Max.

"Well, I think it's time to get started," said Farmer Bob, "so let me give each of you a bucket."

He passed out a bucket to each kid and said, "Remember to make sure you can see someone else at all times."

Max put his bucket on his head. "Help! Help! I can't see anyone!" he said. His voice echoed inside the bucket.

"Max," said Mrs. Wushy, "if you're going to fool around and not be a good listener, then you're just going to have to wait with me."

Max quickly took the bucket off his head. He didn't want to miss his chance to find the wooden apple.

"All right, if everyone is ready," said Farmer Bob, "on your mark, get set, go!"

We all went running into the trees.

"Oh, look at this big juicy apple," said Jessie. "I don't think I've ever seen such a big apple before."

"That one really is huge!" said Robbie.

"I definitely want to take this one home to show my mom and my *abuela,* my grandma," said Jessie. "They are not going to believe it!"

Jessie gently twisted the apple off the branch just like Farmer Bob had done.

"You did that perfectly," said Farmer Bob. "Just like a real apple farmer."

Jessie smiled.

"I want that one way up there," Chloe whined. "But I can't reach it."

"Would you like me to lift you up?" asked Farmer Bob.

"Yes, please," said Chloe. "But be careful. This is a new dress, and my mom doesn't want me to get it dirty."

Farmer Bob shook his head and lifted Chloe

so she could pick the apple way up high in the tree.

"Oh no!" said Chloe.

"What's wrong?" said Farmer Bob.

"I thought this was the wooden apple, but it isn't, and now I've broken one of my fingernails.

I had them painted candy-apple red just for this trip."

Farmer Bob laughed. "You certainly are a city girl, aren't you?"

"I don't think the wooden apple is right here," I said. "I'm going to walk down there a little bit. Want to come, Robbie?"

"Sure," Robbie said.

We walked past a few trees, and then I whispered, "I think I see it. Come on!"

CHAPTER 6

Lost!

I ran toward a tree, but just as I was about to grab the apple, Max appeared from nowhere and shoved me out of the way. I flew to the ground, and Max grabbed the apple.

"I got it! I got it!" Max yelled.

Robbie ran over to me. "Are you all right?" he asked.

"Yeah," I said, trying to sit up. "Where did he come from?"

"I don't know. Out from behind that tree, I think."

"What a cheater. He's been spying on us the whole time!"

Robbie gave me his hand and helped me up. I brushed the dirt off my pants.

Max looked at the apple, and then he just dropped it onto the ground.

"I guess that wasn't the wooden apple," said Robbie.

"Good. Serves him right. That's what he gets for being a bully and a cheater," I said.

Jessie ran over. "Are you OK, Freddy? What happened?"

"I thought I had found the wooden apple, so I was running to get it, but then Max pushed me down so that he could get there first."

"You're just a big bully, Max Sellars!" Jessie yelled. "And cheaters never win!"

"Let's go somewhere else and get away from him," I said.

"Good idea," said Robbie. "Want to come with us, Jessie?"

"No, thanks. I saw a perfect apple over there. I'm going to go back and get it."

"OK, we'll see you in a little bit," I said.

Robbie and I walked about two rows over. "How about if you go that way, and I go this way?" I said.

"All right," said Robbie. "That sounds like a good plan."

Robbie started walking to the right, and I went to the left. I swung my bucket and hummed a little song to myself. I really wanted to find that wooden apple and win the five dollars. There was a cool shark's tooth at Timeless Treasures at the mall that I had been saving up for. If I won the five dollars, I would probably have enough money to go buy it that weekend.

"See anything yet?" Robbie yelled.

"Nope! Not yet!" I yelled back. But I did find the perfect apple. It was just right for my mom's apple crisp. I gently twisted it off the branch and dropped it into my bucket. I smacked my lips and rubbed my stomach. Fresh homemade apple crisp. Yum!

I walked a little farther and froze in my tracks. "There it is," I whispered to myself. "The wooden apple. I'm going to be rich!" My heart skipped a beat.

I ran over to the tree and tried to grab the apple, but it was just out of reach. I hit my forehead with my palm. "Think, think, think."

Maybe if I turned the bucket upside down and stood on it, I'd be able to reach the apple. I had to move quickly before anyone saw me. Who knew where Max was? I kept thinking he was going to come out of nowhere and knock me to the ground again.

I dumped the apples out of my bucket, turned it over, and stood on top. Bingo! I could just get my fingers around the apple. I gave it a little twist, and the apple fell off into my hand.

My heart sank. It wasn't the wooden apple after all. Just a plain old piece of fruit.

"Found anything yet?" I called to Robbie.

"Not yet!" he called back.

I was starting to get discouraged. Where could this wooden apple be? I decided to walk over one more row.

I stopped at each tree and carefully looked up into the branches, hoping to find the wooden apple, but no luck. I walked a little farther, picked a few more apples, and put them into my bucket.

"Anything yet?" I yelled to Robbie.

No answer.

"Anything yet?" I yelled again.

Still no answer.

"That's weird," I thought. "Why didn't he answer me?"

I walked out from underneath the tree branches and looked down the row of trees to the right. I didn't see anyone.

Then I looked down the row of the trees to the left. No one was there, either.

"Hello?" I called. No one answered.

My heart started to beat a little bit faster.

Where was everyone?

I looked up and down the row again, but I didn't see or hear anyone.

"Oh no! Oh no!" I thought. "I didn't follow

rule number one. I was supposed to make sure I could see someone at all times, but right now I can't see anybody. Where did Robbie go?"

I was starting to panic. All the trees looked the same. I had no idea how to get back to the hay cart. I was lost in the orchard!

CHAPTER 7

What's That Noise?

Everywhere I looked, all I saw was trees . . . trees . . . trees! But no people! I stood perfectly still and listened. I couldn't hear any voices. All I could hear was the loud beating of my heart.

My stomach started to do flip-flops. What if they couldn't find me, and I had to spend the night out here in the dark all by myself?

Maybe a bear would come out of the woods looking for food and eat me up!

Now I was really scaring myself. I had to find my way out of there . . . and fast!

I started to walk in one direction but nothing looked familiar, so I turned around and went back the other way.

I had walked down one whole row when I heard the noise.

It was like a quiet sniffling. It seemed to be coming from behind a tree. I tiptoed slowly around the other side of the tree, and there was Max!

He was sitting down at the base of the tree with his head in his hands. And what was that noise? Was he crying? Was the biggest bully in the whole first grade actually crying?

As soon as he heard me, he jumped up and quickly wiped his face with his hand. "Uh, Freddy, what are you doing here?" he said.

"What are *you* doing here?" I said.

"I . . . um . . . was . . . just . . . taking a break," said Max.

"Really?" I said. "Because it sounded to me like you were crying."

"Crying? Me? No!" said Max.

"Well, I'm glad I found you," I said to Max. I had never thought I'd ever say those words to him in my whole life, but right now I was happy to see anyone, even Max Sellars.

"Really?" said Max.

"Yeah," I said, "because I'm lost. I was trying so hard to find that wooden apple that I didn't realize I had wandered so far away from the group."

"If I tell you something, do you promise not to tell anyone?" said Max.

"Yeah . . . sure," I said.

"I'm lost, too!" said Max.

"Are you scared?" I asked.

At first Max didn't answer me, but he looked scared, and I was sure I had heard him crying.

"How about you, Freddy? Are you scared?"

"A little bit," I said.

"Me, too," said Max. "I think we should stick together. We can help each other find the way out."

I didn't think Max even knew how to help someone else. He was always hurting people, not helping them, but I definitely did not want to be alone. "OK," I said. "Let's stick together and find our way out."

"Which way should we go?" said Max.

"Do you see any footprints?" I asked.

"Yeah, right there," said Max, pointing to some footprints right next to the tree.

"Those won't help us," I said.

"Why not?" said Max.

"Because they are *our* footprints."

"How do you know?"

"Lift up your foot. See how they match the marks on the bottom of your shoe?" I said.

"Wow! You're like a real detective!" Max said.

"Thanks," I said, and smiled. "Do you see any other footprints?"

"Hey, look! Over there!" Max said, pointing to the left.

"Those look like the bottom of Chloe's fancy red shoes," I said. "Let's follow those. I bet they will lead us out of here."

We followed the footsteps for a while down one row and then another, but we still did not find the group.

Max stopped and glared at me. "OK, Shark Boy, do you have any other ideas? That one didn't work."

I couldn't believe he was getting angry with me. He wasn't coming up with any ideas of his own. "How about you?" I said. "Do you have any ideas?"

"Well . . . um . . . we . . . could . . . um . . . ," Max stammered.

"Thanks, Max! Those are great ideas," I said.

I had to think of something, and I had to think

of it fast. Time was running out. I sat down on my bucket like I had before, and hit my forehead with my palm. "Think, think, think."

"What are you doing, Weirdo?" Max said.

"I'm thinking. I'm trying to think of a way to get us out of here!"

Just then Max kicked my bucket, and it gave me a great idea.

"Why didn't I think of that before?" I said to myself.

"Think of what?" asked Max.

"Making noise with the buckets," I said. "Pick up your bucket and start pounding on it like a drum. If we make a lot of noise, I'm sure the rest of the class will hear us!"

We both picked up our buckets and started pounding wildly on them with some sticks we found. It made a really loud noise. "They must be able to hear this," I said.

We walked a little farther, banging our buckets, and then I thought I heard a voice.

“Shhhhh,” I said to Max. “Listen.”

We stopped banging for a minute, and sure enough, we heard Mrs. Wushy’s voice. “Max? Freddy? Is that you?”

We banged our buckets again. “We’re over here!” we yelled. “Over here!”

Then I heard Robbie’s voice. “They’re over there, Mrs. Wushy. I can see Freddy’s red sweatshirt. Good thing that bright red doesn’t blend in with the green trees!”

Mrs. Wushy, Farmer Bob, and the whole class came running up to us.

“Are you OK? Are you OK?” they all asked.

“Yes,” we said.

“That must have been really scary,” said Chloe.

“Were you scared? Were you scared?” all the kids asked.

Max looked at me, and I looked at him. “Uh, no . . . we weren’t scared at all,” we said.

"Oh my goodness! I was so worried. I had no idea where you boys were," said Mrs. Wushy.

"I'm glad you boys are OK," said Farmer Bob. "But I am very disappointed that you did not follow my rules. I have those rules to keep everyone safe."

Max and I hung our heads.

"I think you owe Farmer Bob an apology," said Mrs. Wushy.

"I'm sorry, Farmer Bob," I said, "for not following your rules."

Max just stood there. He didn't say anything.

"Max," said Mrs. Wushy, "we are waiting."

Max kicked the dirt.

"Now, Max," said Mrs. Wushy.

"I'm sorry," Max mumbled.

"Of course I am going to talk to your parents about this, boys," said Mrs. Wushy. "I know they will not be very happy."

"Not very happy! My mom is going to be really angry," I whispered to Robbie. "I know

I'm going to be in big trouble. It's just that I wanted to find the wooden apple so badly."

"Hey," said Max. "Did anyone find the wooden apple?"

"Yes," said Mrs. Wushy.

"Who?" he said.

Jessie got a big grin on her face. "Me!"

"No way!" said Max.

"Yes way!" said Jessie. "You got beat by a girl, Max Sellars."

Max looked away and kicked the dirt again.

"Just like I told you," said Chloe with her hands on her hips, "cheaters never win!"

"Congratulations, Jessie," I said, patting her on the back. "I am so happy for you."

"Thanks, Freddy," said Jessie.

"What are you going to do with the money?"

"I don't know yet," said Jessie. "Five dollars is a lot of money!"

"Well, now that we have everybody back safe and sound, how about we all go back to the old

barn and make some fresh apple cider?" said Farmer Bob.

"Cider! Cider!" we all chanted as we gathered our buckets of apples and climbed back onto the hay cart.

"Giddyup, Sugar!" said Farmer Bob. "Take us to the old barn!"

CHAPTER 8

Cider and Doughnuts

When we got back to the old barn, Farmer Bob said, “Everybody, bring two apples from your bucket and follow me.”

I put my bucket on the ground and fished around for two of the biggest, juiciest apples I could find. Then I followed him into the old barn.

“Throw your two apples into this big bin here, and we’ll make some fresh apple cider,” said Farmer Bob.

We all threw our apples into the bin, except for Chloe. She complained that she couldn't throw that far, so Farmer Bob lifted her up so she could drop hers in. Then we watched in amazement as the old cider press turned our big juicy apples into fresh apple cider.

Farmer Bob turned a faucet on the cooling tank, and the apple cider poured out into a jug.

"Come on outside, everybody," said Farmer Bob. "We'll drink our cider and have a treat."

"Treats! Oh, I just love treats!" said Chloe, jumping up and down.

"Stop bouncing around like a bunny rabbit," said Max.

"Oh, be quiet, Max," said Chloe. "You're just mad you didn't find the wooden apple."

We all followed Farmer Bob outside. "Come sit down on the picnic tables over here," he said.

Everybody ran to get a seat. When Max tried to squeeze in, he gave Chloe a shove, and she flew off the bench and fell into the dirt.

"Wahhhh! Wahhhh!" she sobbed. "Look what you did, Max. Now my new dress is all dirty."

Mrs. Wushy ran over. "What happened?" she said.

"Max pushed me off the bench and now my new dress is all dirty," Chloe wailed. "My mom told me to keep it clean."

Mrs. Wushy helped Chloe up, brushed off her dress, and then turned to Max. "How many times have I told you not to push people? I think you'd better come sit with me." She grabbed Max's hand, and they sat down at the other end of the bench, right next to me.

Farmer Bob brought over a cup of cider for each of us. "Here you go. Fresh cider right from the cider press. How does it taste?"

We all took a sip.

"This is delicious!" said Jessie. "It tastes like I'm drinking fresh apples."

"This is the best cider I have ever had," said Robbie, smacking his lips.

"Wait until you taste this," said Farmer Bob, pointing to a box he was holding in his hand.

"What is it?" asked Robbie.

"Is it the treat?" asked Chloe.

"It is a fresh homemade cider doughnut," said Farmer Bob, lifting one out of the box.

"Cider doughnuts! I've never had one before," Jessie said.

"Well then, you are in for a treat," said Farmer Bob. "My grandfather used to make them for me when I was your age. I couldn't wait for apple-picking time just so my grandfather would make me warm cider doughnuts."

Farmer Bob passed out a doughnut to each of us. "Go on. Take a bite. Tell me what you think."

I bit into mine. It was warm, and brown, and sugary. It almost melted in my mouth. "Yum!" I said, licking the sugar off my lips.

"This is awesome!" said Jessie.

"Yum, yummy, yum!" said Robbie, smiling and patting his tummy.

"What do we all say to Farmer Bob?" said Mrs. Wushy.

"Thank you, Farmer Bob," we all said.

"Well, I hope you boys and girls had fun here today at Apple Hill Orchard."

"I had a great day," said Jessie.

"Me, too!" said Robbie. "How about you, Freddy?"

I turned to look at Max, and he looked at me. "It will definitely be a day I will never forget!" I said. Then I took another bite of my cider doughnut and smiled.

DEAR READER,

I am a kindergarten and first-grade teacher. I used to live and teach in California, and my school wasn't near an apple orchard. Now I live in Vermont and there are lots of apple orchards really close to my school. This year I took my class to an apple orchard for the very first time.

We all had so much fun. Just like Freddy's class, we got to watch a real cider press making apple cider, and then we tasted the fresh cider. It was delicious. We also got to taste homemade cider doughnuts. They were warm, and sugary, and yummy!

Everyone got a bucket to fill with apples from the orchard. Luckily, no one got lost in the orchard like Freddy and Max did. We took the apples back to our classroom and made apple crisp. (The recipe is in the back of this book!)

Have you ever been to an apple orchard with

your class or your family? I'd love to hear about it.

Just write to me at:

Ready, Freddy! Fun Stuff
c/o Scholastic Inc.
P.O. Box 711
New York, NY 10013-0711

I hope you have as much fun reading *Apple Orchard Race* as I had writing it.

HAPPY READING!

Freddy's Fun Pages

FREDDY'S SHARK JOURNAL

THE SHARK'S BODY

There are more than 460 species of shark, but most sharks have certain things in common. Every shark has:

- a mouthful of teeth.
- five to seven gill slits on each side of its body. It uses these to breathe.
- a dorsal fin to help with balance and steering.
- pectoral fins, which help the shark stop.
- a caudal fin, which keeps the shark from tipping over in the water.
- a snout with nostrils.
- skin that feels rough, like sandpaper.

APPLE CRISP RECIPE

Would you like to taste the delicious apple crisp that Freddy's mom makes? Just try this simple recipe below. Be sure to have an adult help you with this one!

INGREDIENTS:

5 apples
1/4 cup water
1 teaspoon cinnamon
1/3 cup melted butter
3/4 cup flour
1 cup sugar
foil pan (8x8 inches)

DIRECTIONS:

1. Grease the bottom of your pan.

2. Wash and peel 5 apples, then cut them into slices.

3. Lay the apple slices in the bottom of your pan.

4. Pour 1/4 cup of water on top of the apples and sprinkle them with 1 teaspoon of cinnamon.

5. Mix together 1/3 cup of melted butter, 3/4 cup of flour, and 1 cup of sugar.

6. Sprinkle the mixture on top of the apples.

7. Bake at 350 degrees for 45–50 minutes or until the top is light brown.

8. ***ENJOY!***

LOST IN THE ORCHARD!

Freddy is lost in the orchard.
Can you help him find
his way out?

FUNNY FRUITS!

Here are some of Freddy's favorite apple jokes. Try them on your friends and family!

1. What kind of apple isn't an apple?

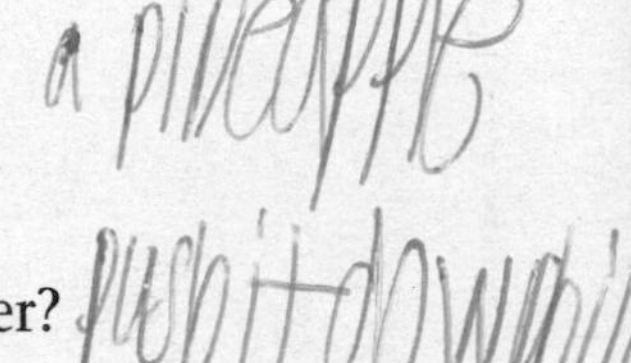

2. How do you make an apple turnover?

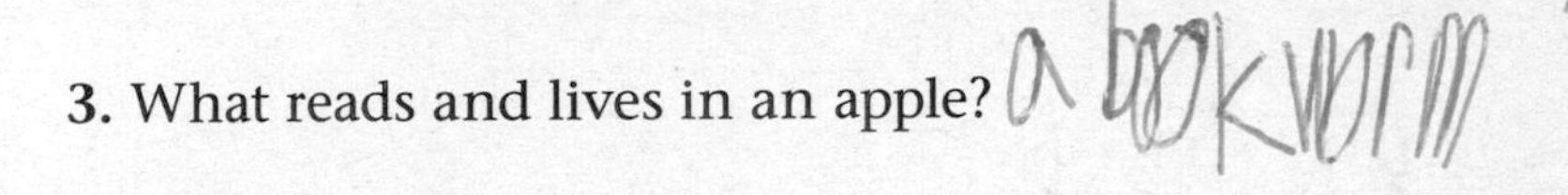

3. What reads and lives in an apple?

1. A pineapple   2. Push it downhill.   3. A bookworm

APPLE ART ACTIVITY

You can make stamps out of apples! Just follow these simple directions.

YOU WILL NEED:

apples
paint (whatever colors you like)
art paper
paper plates
markers

DIRECTIONS:

1. Ask an adult to cut each of your apples in half.

2. Pour some paint onto a paper plate.

3. Dip the flat side of your apple into the paint, and then press it down onto your art paper.

4. You can either make designs or turn the apple prints into pictures by adding to them with markers. For example, you can make a butterfly by adding two antennae to the top of the apple print.

5. You can also make apple prints all over a piece of paper and then use the paper to wrap a gift.

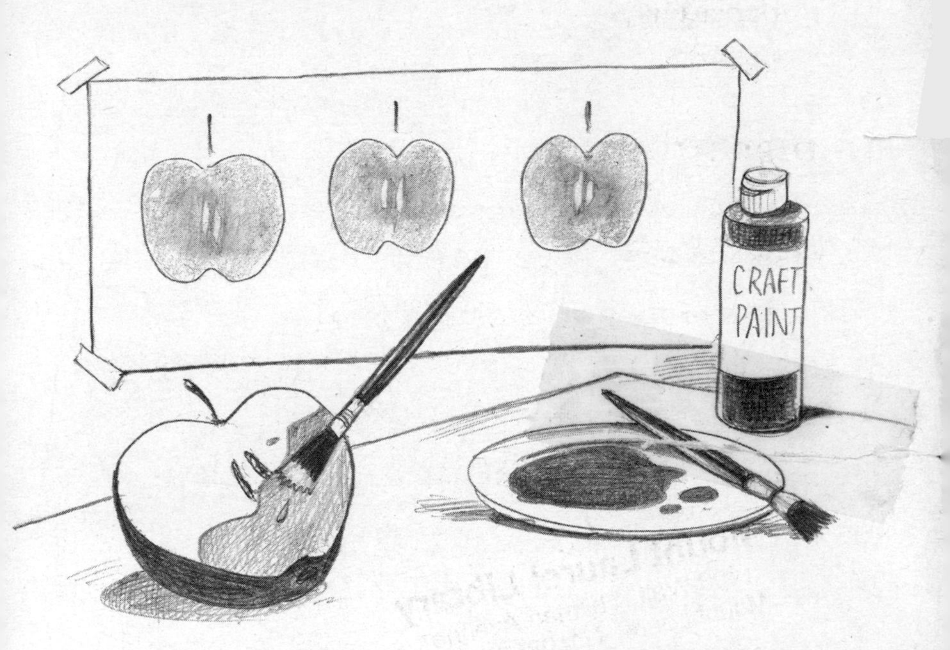

Just use your imagination and have fun!

Have you read all about Freddy?

Don't miss any of Freddy's funny adventures!